Ella's New Hat

and her

Terrible Cat

Written and Illustrated by Pamela Grandstaff

For Ella Rose

Ella bought a bright blue hat,
and took it home to show her cat.

"The crown's too high and the brim's too flat,"
said Ella's mean and terrible cat.

Ella tried this and that
to improve the look of her new hat.
She bought a ribbon in satiny pink.
"It looks much better," she did think.

"What were you thinking when you did that?"
said Ella's rotten, horrible cat

Ella thought buttons
might make it look better,
So she took a green one
off an old sweater.
She found an orange one
in a jar in the shed,
And in her junk drawer
she found bright shiny red.

"People will laugh if you go out in that."
said Ella's dreadful, difficult cat.

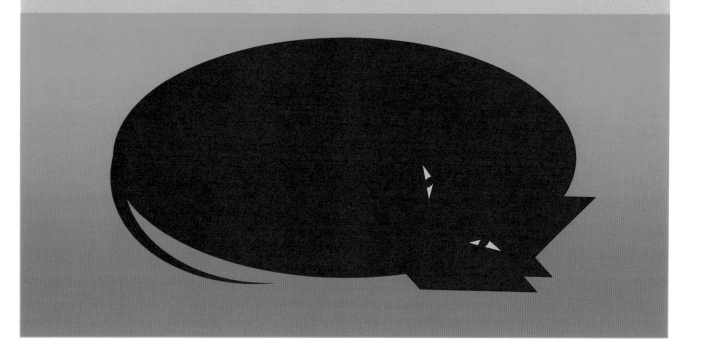

Ella cut fringe off
an old chenille bedspread,
And added it to the
blue hat brim instead.
It bobbled and danced
each time that she shook.
Quite taken was Ella
with this brand new look.

"Fringe is not something one puts on a hat,"
said Ella's contrary, disagreeable cat.

Out in the garden were
flowers so pretty,
Ella felt sure they
would please her smug kitty.
She gathered the blossoms
before she ate lunch,
Then dressed up her hat
with the best of the bunch.

"You try way too hard and you always fall flat,"
said Ella's thoroughly unpleasant cat.

Some butterflies were in a flutter;
One showed up and then another.
One landed on the bright blue rim,
One tap-danced on the hat's wide brim.

"Some people don't look good in hats,"
said Ella's obnoxious, despicable cat.

Ella asked some buzzing bees,
"Would you join my hat, too, please?"
The bees were tempted by the fest.
"Have fun," said Ella. "Join the rest."

"Too bad it makes you look so fat,"
said Ella's wicked, malicious cat.

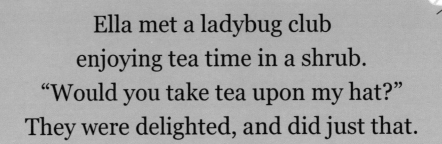

Ella met a ladybug club
enjoying tea time in a shrub.
"Would you take tea upon my hat?"
They were delighted, and did just that.

"You're kidding, right, about that hat?"
said Ella's heartless, hateful cat.

Some dragonflies went flying by,
zigging, zagging in the sky.
They circled once and then came down,
and settled on the blue hat crown.

"You're not really going out in that,"
said Ella's cruel and spiteful cat.

Ella asked a bird of blue
if it would care to join them, too.
"I'd love to share the hat with you!"
it said with glee, like bluebirds do.

"No one worth knowing would ever wear that,"
said Ella's vile and vicious cat.

Ella met some lively crickets
playing music, selling tickets.
They set up on the tippy top,
and played some blue grass punk hip hop.

"I'd rather eat stinkbugs than listen to that,"
said Ella's rude, persnickety cat.

Ella asked some grasshopper brothers
if they would like to join the others.
The brothers brought a drum and fiddle,
and joined the crickets in the middle.

"I prefer Bartók played in E flat,"
said Ella's snobby, pretentious cat.

The neighbors came and brought their cats,
and wore their funniest, wildest hats.
The spent the sunny afternoon
dancing, laughing, and singing tunes.
In Ella's garden they all played
bingo, croquet, and charades.

Inside the cat amused itself
by knocking dishes off the shelf.
The party seemed like lots of fun
but the cat just hated everyone.
It threw a fit and hissed and spat,
"This is all the fault of that dumb hat!"

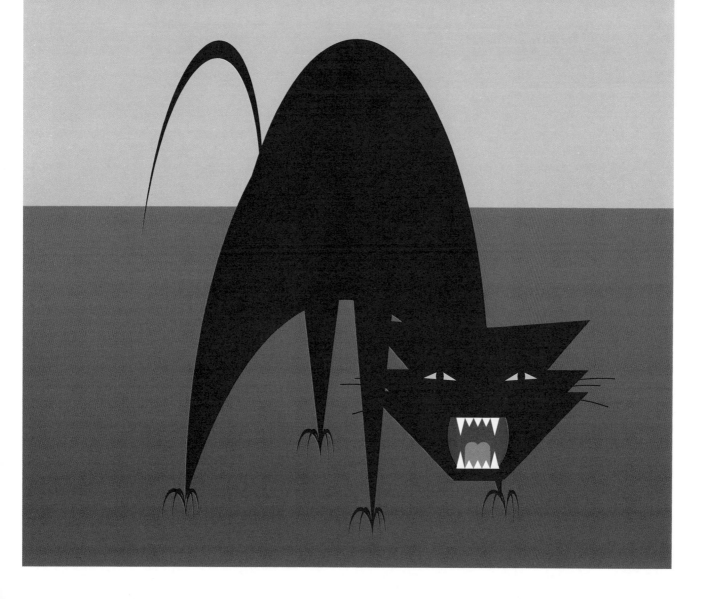

But there was no one there to listen
to its bad-tempered fit of hissin'.
The cat discovered it's no fun
to be ignored by everyone.
People tend to stay away
if you only have mean things to say.
A pathetic fit, poorly thrown,
left Ella's cat all alone.

The party lasted very late,
and everyone said it was great.
When Ella came in tired and glad
she saw her cat was pouting sad.

Ella said, "I don't want to chat
about what you think of my new hat.
You could have joined us in the garden
if only you had begged my pardon."

She put her hat upon a chair,
then took a bath and washed her hair.
"Too bad," she told the bad cat, later,
"You missed the fun, you mean hat-hater."

After Ella went to bed,
Cat put the hat upon its head;
It looked into the dresser mirror,
and thought the hat looked so much dearer.

"I think it just looks bad on her,
because she doesn't have my fur.
Too bad I have to shred this hat;
It looks much better on a cat."

Which goes to show, among many things,
this cat did not learn anything.

If your new hat makes you glad
but some mean cat says it looks bad,
Wear your beautiful, wonderful hat,
then hide it from that no-good cat.

The End

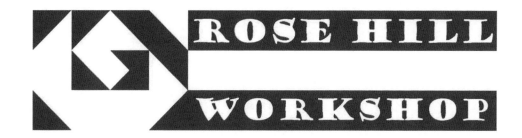

Pamela Grandstaff created this book for Ella Rose, her smart, beautiful, and witty niece.

Pamela loves all cats despite their repeated attempts to undermine her self-confidence.

She has written another book for children, *June Bug Days and Firefly Nights,* as well as the *Rose Hill Mystery* series for silly grownups.

Find out more at RoseHillWorkshop.com

June Bug Days
and
Firefly Nights

**Written and Illustrated by
Pamela Grandstaff**

Available at Amazon.com, Barnes & Noble,
Kobo Books, Sony eBooks and Apple iBooks.

Proof

Made in the USA
Charleston, SC
07 July 2011

Ella's New Hat

Ella has purchased a bright blue hat that she thinks is beautiful, but her bad-tempered, disagreeable cat doesn't like it.

No matter what Ella does to improve her new hat, by decorating it with ribbons and buttons, or by inviting ladybugs to have tea upon the brim, her cantankerous cat refuses to approve.

When Ella wears her hat anyway and has great time as a result, her persnickety cat throws a fit and pouts, but everyone else is having too much fun to notice.

A humorous reminder that you can't please everyone so you might as well please yourself; anyone who has a persnickety friend or family member will enjoy this funny story.

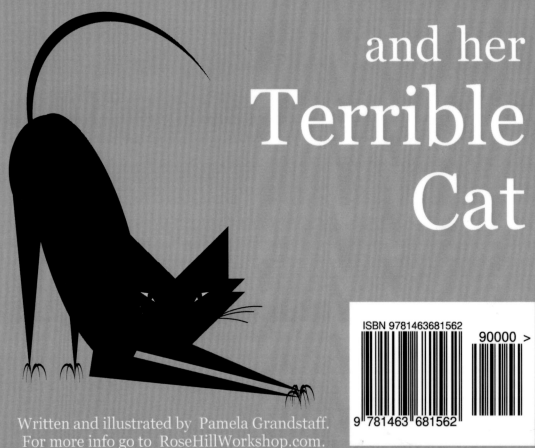

and her
Terrible
Cat

ISBN 9781463681562

Written and illustrated by Pamela Grandstaff.
For more info go to RoseHillWorkshop.com.

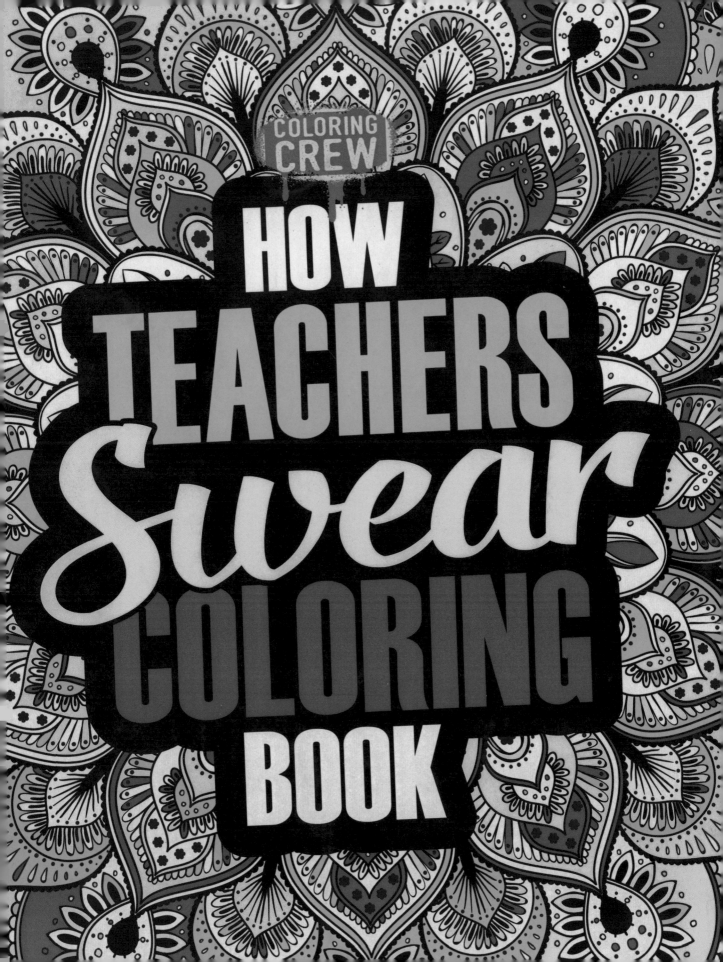